Published by Grolier Books
© 1996 Disney Enterprises, Inc.
No portion of this book may be
reproduced without the written
consent of Disney Enterprises, Inc.
Produced by Bumpy Slide Books
Adapted by Lisa Ann Marsoli
Illustrations by Arkadia Illustrations Ltd.
Designed by Vickey Bolling
Printed in the United States of America
ISBN: 0-7171-8755-6

GROLIER
BOOK CLUB EDITION

grabah was abuzz with excitement. Aladdin and Jasmine's wedding day was finally here! The Genie was busy attending to important details — such as parking the camels. Iago was busy inspecting the lavish gifts. And the Sultan was rushing about nervously, like any father of the bride.

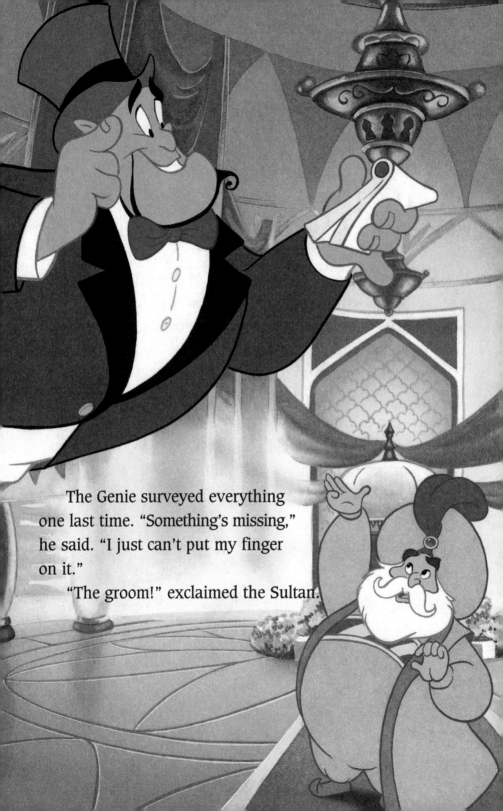

The Genie surveyed everything one last time. "Something's missing," he said. "I just can't put my finger on it."

"The groom!" exclaimed the Sultan.

The Genie headed straight for Aladdin's place. "Excuse me!" he shouted. "But somebody's going to be late for his own wedding!"

"Hold on, Genie, there's something I need," replied Aladdin. He opened an old wooden box. Inside was a dagger decorated with a golden hand. "It belonged to my father," Aladdin said softly.

The Genie was surprised. "You've never said a word about your father," he said.

"He died a long time ago," explained Aladdin. "Maybe he could have shown me how to be a good husband. What if I'm no good at it?"

"If your father were here, he'd be as proud of you as I am," the Genie reassured him. "Now let's get out of here. We've got a wedding to go to!"

As the wedding hour drew closer, an odd
collection of men slipped in with the guests. They
were the Forty Thieves! Cassim, the King of Thieves,
was their leader. He had come in search of one of
the couple's gifts — a magic scepter. No one noticed
the thieves, because everyone was waiting for the
arrival of the bride.

At last, Jasmine appeared. The guests watched as the beautiful princess walked down the aisle.

"Well, we're finally here," said Aladdin as the two joined hands.

"Together forever," Jasmine added, smiling.

Meanwhile, the thieves were eyeing the gifts.

"You create a distraction," Cassim instructed a thief named Sa'luk. Sa'luk hated Cassim because he wanted to be the King of Thieves himself. But Sa'luk did as he was told and started an elephant stampede.

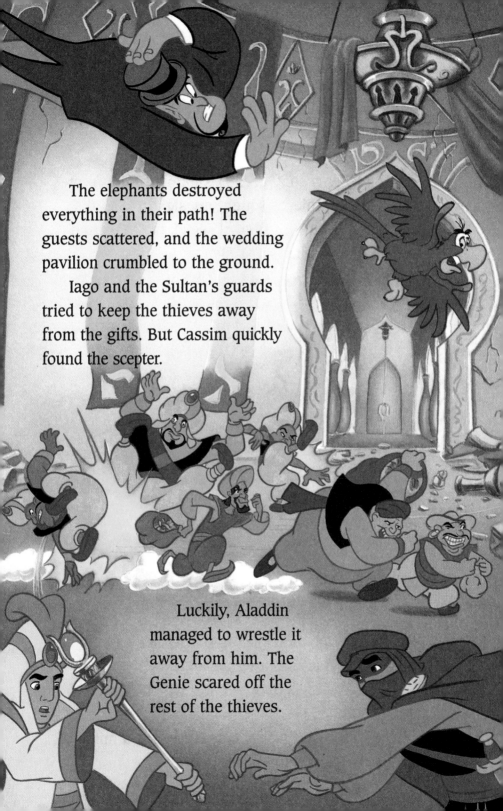

The elephants destroyed everything in their path! The guests scattered, and the wedding pavilion crumbled to the ground.

Iago and the Sultan's guards tried to keep the thieves away from the gifts. But Cassim quickly found the scepter.

Luckily, Aladdin managed to wrestle it away from him. The Genie scared off the rest of the thieves.

Aladdin and Jasmine surveyed the ruins of the wedding pavilion. "What were they after?" the princess asked.

Suddenly, a shaft of light shot out of the scepter. "The King of Thieves sought my sight to find the *ultimate* treasure," it said. "I see all that has been and all that will be."

The scepter contained an oracle that could answer any question it was asked.

"You could ask about your past," Jasmine told Aladdin.

"My past isn't just one question. It's a million questions," Aladdin replied.

"Ahh, but mere questions about your past can be answered by your father," the oracle said. It showed them the blurred image of a man's face.

"My father is alive?" repeated Aladdin, not sure how to feel.

"Follow the trail of the Forty Thieves," it told him. "Your father is trapped within their world."

Thinking that his father was the thieves' prisoner, Aladdin bid Jasmine good-bye. Then he flew off on the Magic Carpet with Abu and Iago.

The thieves' trail was fresh, and the three followed it to a beach. They watched as Cassim called, "Open, Sesame!" The water parted, and so did the cliffs on the other side of the bay!

The thieves galloped into the opening. Aladdin, Abu, and Iago managed to swoop inside before the rock slammed shut again.

Inside the cavern were the ruins of an ancient city — and the home of the Forty Thieves.

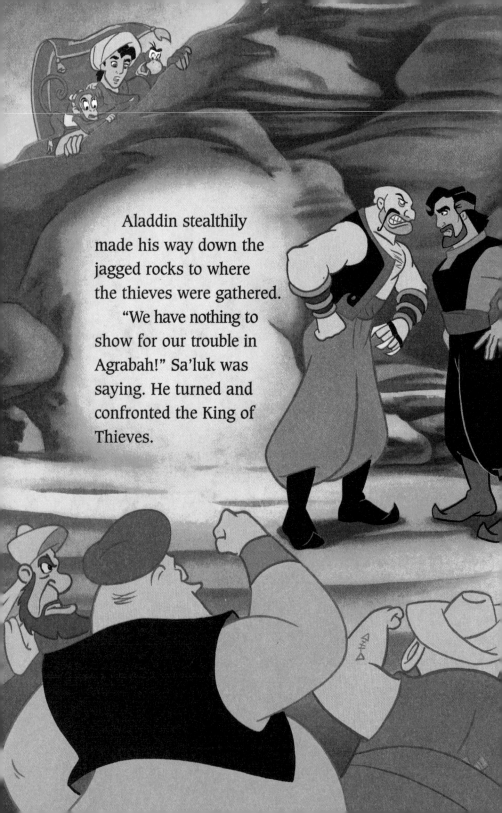

Aladdin stealthily made his way down the jagged rocks to where the thieves were gathered.

"We have nothing to show for our trouble in Agrabah!" Sa'luk was saying. He turned and confronted the King of Thieves.

Suddenly, Aladdin recognized Cassim — the King of Thieves was his father!

Sa'luk raised his tiger claw to swipe at Cassim. But in an instant, Sa'luk was thrown to the ground.

"Run!" yelled Aladdin. "I've got him!" Cassim looked confused. Why was the stranger helping him?

"I'm Aladdin! You're my father," Aladdin explained.

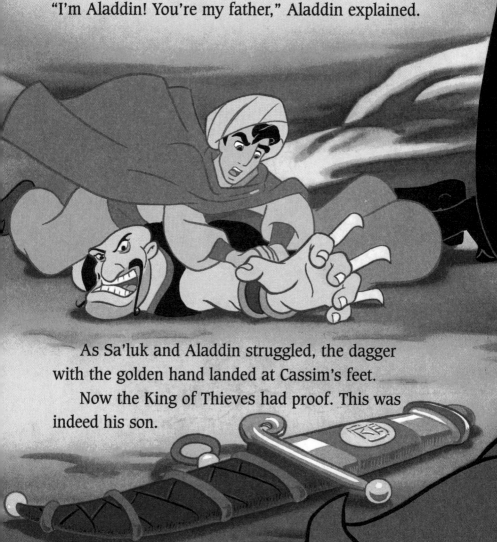

As Sa'luk and Aladdin struggled, the dagger with the golden hand landed at Cassim's feet.

Now the King of Thieves had proof. This was indeed his son.

Sa'luk told the others that Aladdin and his friends must die. But Cassim persuaded them to allow Aladdin to fight Sa'luk. If Aladdin won, he could become one of the thieves.

A storm was raging as the two began their battle atop the cliffs. At first it looked as if Sa'luk would win.

But Aladdin fought harder and harder, finally sending Sa'luk over the edge of the cliff.

"Imagine! Losing an enemy and gaining a son in the same day!" Cassim rejoiced. Then he took his son to his secret lair.

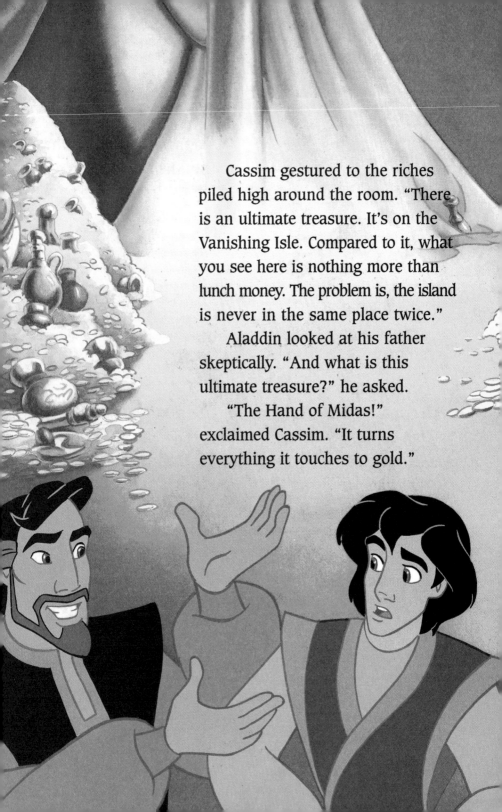

Cassim gestured to the riches piled high around the room. "There is an ultimate treasure. It's on the Vanishing Isle. Compared to it, what you see here is nothing more than lunch money. The problem is, the island is never in the same place twice."

Aladdin looked at his father skeptically. "And what is this ultimate treasure?" he asked.

"The Hand of Midas!" exclaimed Cassim. "It turns everything it touches to gold."

"That's why I left your mother," Aladdin's father continued. "I wanted you to have everything, and the Hand of Midas was the only way."

"I didn't want gold, I wanted a father," Aladdin said gently. "I still want one."

Cassim shook his head. "It's been so long, I wouldn't know where to begin," he admitted.

"Well, you can start by coming to my wedding!" said Aladdin.

What they didn't know was that Sa'luk had survived his fall from the cliff and was on his way to Agrabah.

The thief met with Rasoul, the captain of the Sultan's guards. Sa'luk told Rasoul the location of the thieves' hideout — and the magic phrase to open the cave.

At dawn, Rasoul and the other guards arrived on the beach.

"Open, Caraway!" Rasoul thundered. Nothing happened. "Didn't you say it was 'Open, Sesame'?" Fazal reminded him.

The sea parted, and the Sultan's men soon
reached the hideout. They surprised the thieves
and took most of them as prisoners. But Rasoul was
disappointed, for Cassim was nowhere to be found.

That's because the King of
Thieves had gone back to Agrabah
with Aladdin to meet everyone before
the wedding. Cassim was surprised to
find that Aladdin had a genie. The
Genie was surprised to learn that the
King of Thieves was Aladdin's father!

Next Cassim charmed Jasmine and the Sultan. He let them think that he had been a prisoner of the Forty Thieves. He certainly didn't want them to know he was responsible for ruining the last wedding!

Soon everyone went to get ready for the wedding.
While Cassim dressed, Iago begged him to break
into the royal treasury and steal the oracle.

"I promise you, bird, after this I go straight,"
vowed Cassim.

Aladdin and Jasmine were ready to begin
the ceremony. But Aladdin's father was nowhere
to be seen — until Rasoul dragged him in, bound
in chains.

"Your Majesty, meet the King of Thieves!"
Rasoul announced. "We caught him trying to
steal again."

Aladdin's feelings were hurt. "Now I know why you *really* came back," he said to his dad.

"Your father is the *leader* of the Forty Thieves?" the Sultan asked in disbelief.

"Aladdin, did you know who he was?" asked Jasmine.

Aladdin faced her, saying, "I thought I could change him."

Reluctantly, the Sultan sentenced Cassim and Iago to life imprisonment in the dungeon.

Aladdin couldn't change his father. But he also couldn't stand the thought of him trapped in the dungeon forever. So that night, Aladdin broke Cassim out of jail.

Though his father asked Aladdin to go with him, Aladdin let him take the oracle and said good-bye. Aladdin didn't want to leave Jasmine the way his father had left him.

Now Sa'luk had to find another way to rid himself of Cassim. He went to see the thieves who remained at the hideout. They were surprised to see him alive.

"Cassim betrayed you!" Sa'luk told them. "How do you think the guard knew the magic words to part the sea and raid our hideout?"

When Cassim arrived to share the oracle with the thieves, they turned on him and took him and Iago prisoner.

With the oracle promising to show them the way, the thieves went to sea to find the Vanishing Isle. Luckily, Iago managed to escape.

Back at the palace, the Sultan scolded Aladdin for helping his father.

"I'm sorry for what I did," Aladdin apologized. "But I had to help him. What else could I do?"

Jasmine spoke up. "I know I would do the same for my father," she said.

"Let us put this matter behind us," suggested the Sultan. "We have postponed this wedding long enough!"

Just then, Iago flew in and told them what had happened to Cassim. With the Genie following them, Aladdin and his friends hopped on the Magic Carpet and set out to save the King of Thieves.

Out on the sea, the thieves' ship sailed toward a huge
beam of light. Inside the light, the oracle spoke. "You
have arrived," it told them. The oracle and the light
disappeared, leaving the thieves surrounded by fog.

Suddenly the water began to churn around them.
Their craft pitched violently from side to side. Then a
temple began to rise out of the sea.

"The Vanishing Isle!" said Aladdin, awestruck.
"On the back of a giant turtle!" Jasmine gasped.

The thieves went to explore the island. Sa'luk brought Cassim, whose hands were tied behind his back.

Thinking quickly, the Genie swooped down and bumped hard against the turtle. Then, as the island began to shake and rumble, the Genie reported on the action.

While the thieves were thrown off balance, Aladdin confronted Sa'luk, and the thief was knocked unconscious.

Cassim and Aladdin raced higher up into the temple
until they found the statue that contained the Hand of
Midas. Aladdin removed the hand, careful to hold it by
the wrist, and tossed it to his father.

Just then, Sa'luk arrived and threatened Aladdin. Fearing for his son, Cassim gave Sa'luk the Hand of Midas. When Sa'luk took it, he turned to gold and fell into the water that was rising in the temple.

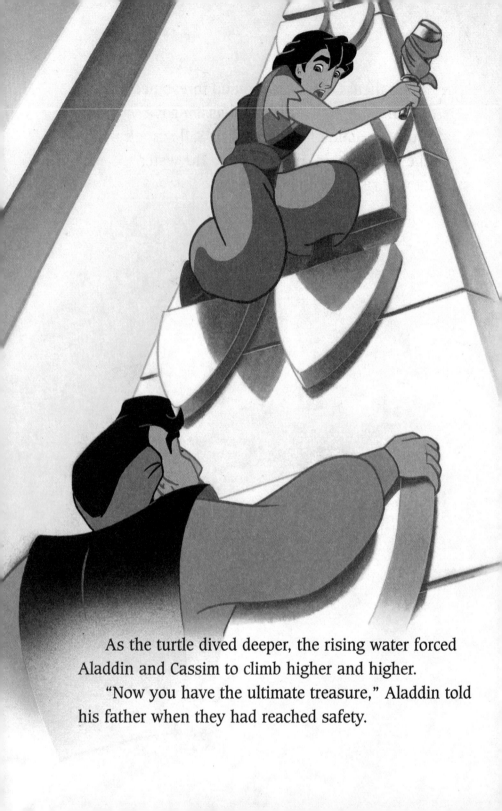

As the turtle dived deeper, the rising water forced
Aladdin and Cassim to climb higher and higher.

"Now you have the ultimate treasure," Aladdin told
his father when they had reached safety.

"No, it almost cost me the ultimate treasure — you," his father replied. Then he tossed the Hand of Midas into the sea.

It landed on the deck of the thieves' ship, turning it to gold. The heavy vessel began to sink as the thieves jumped overboard.

The Magic Carpet took everyone else back to Agrabah.

That very day, to the delight of all, Aladdin and
Jasmine were finally married.

As the newlyweds enjoyed a sunset ride on the
Magic Carpet, they watched Cassim ride off in
search of new adventures. Iago went with him.

Cassim traded his old life as a king of thieves for a new one as the father of a prince. And that suited everyone just fine.